TWISTED FAIRY TALES

OCTO-PUSS IN BOOTS

SAMANTHA NEWMAN

ARCTURUS

This edition published in 2021 by Arcturus Publishing Limited
26/27 Bickels Yard, 151–153 Bermondsey Street,
London SE1 3HA

Written by: Samantha Newman with Joe Harris
Illustrated by: James Hearne
Cover illustration by: Chris Jevons
Designed by: Jeni Child
Edited by: Joe Harris
Art direction: Jessica Holliland

ISBN: 978-1-78888-492-1
CH006617NT
Supplier 13, Date 0421, Print run 10258

Printed in China

Long ago, there lived a young knight called Sir Loin of Beef. Sir Loin was famous for his bravery throughout the kingdom. He was so brave, in fact, that people said he didn't know the meaning of fear. Sir Loin thought that was a bit rude, because he had looked up "fear" in the dictionary, and he was pretty confident that he *did* know what it meant, thank you very much. Sir Loin defeated every monster in the kingdom ... even the mighty ogre, Gutrot.

Sir Loin enjoyed a long and successful career, and grew an impressively bushy beard. However, he eventually grew old and tired of defeating monsters. One day, after vanquishing a sea dragon, he decided to quit. He swam to shore, then marched home, with seaweed—and a determined octopus— still clinging to him.

"Children! I am retiring," Sir Loin announced. "You must now make your own way in the world. Edstrong, my son, take my sword and shield. Anvil, my daughter, to you I give my charger and lance. Use them well!"

Sir Loin's third child, Angus, cleared his throat. "Father, what about me?"

Sir Loin had forgotten about Angus, which was something he often did. He grabbed the octopus that was still holding onto his leg.

"Uh, this is for you, Arnold."

Before Angus could say, "My name isn't Arnold—and what use is an octopus in the big, wide world?" he was thrown out of the front door. It slammed behind him.

"Bye, Angus," called Anvil as she galloped off.

"Enjoy your squid," smirked Edstrong.

Angus grumbled to himself as he trudged away, holding the slimy, squirming octopus.

"This is worse than the time Dad gave me his supper leftovers for my birthday! I hate seafood."

As Angus walked down into town, his eye was caught by the fishmonger's sign. He went inside. "How much will you give me for this stinky, slimy creature?" he asked.

The fishmonger raised an eyebrow. "Is it fresh?"

"I'm fresher than you, old woman!" the octopus piped up.

Angus gasped in shock.

"And you," the octopus pointed a tentacle at Angus, "ought to be more polite. I don't go around saying how revoltingly clean and dry *you* are!"

"I … I don't buy talking fish," the fishmonger spluttered.

"You couldn't afford me anyway," the octopus sniffed. Angus had no words at all. He turned and stumbled back outside.

Angus put the creature down and walked away, but it slithered after him. It soon became clear that Angus' new friend could not only talk—he could also moan. And groan. And grumble.

"My poor tentacles!" cried Octopus, "They're all sore from this hard, scratchy ground."

"So go back to the ocean and swim!" Angus called over his shoulder.

"I don't like the ocean!" Octopus pouted. "It's too wet and cold. And no one talks to me down there. Help me to make my way on land, and I'll help you in return."

Angus sighed and opened his satchel. "Here, I have a spare pair of boots."

"Oh, thank you SO much!" said Octopus. "And could I wear your hat too? I like that jaunty feather."

Angus sighed again and handed it over.

"Now that I'm dressed," Octopus beamed, tipping the hat with one tentacle. "I'm going to help you make a fortune. Let's ask if they need help in the inn across the street."

Angus frowned. "But, what if the innkeeper doesn't like talking octopuses either?"

"Don't worry— he won't know I'm here." Octopus' skin changed from orange to yellow, then from yellow to beige—until he exactly matched the shade of the wall behind him.

Angus knocked on the door of the inn and asked the innkeeper for a job.

The innkeeper led the way to a room that was stacked to the ceiling with dirty dishes. "My dishwashing boy is off work with the plague at the moment," he explained. "I'll pay you a copper coin if you can get all of this clean by the end of the day."

Angus was just about to reply, when the

invisible octopus piped up, doing an
uncanny imitation of Angus' voice.

"I'll get it done in ten minutes, if you pay
me ten gold pieces," said Octopus.

"Ten minutes?" laughed the innkeeper.
"That's impossible. If you can do it that
quickly, I'll eat my hat!"

As soon as the innkeeper left the room,
Octopus leaped into action. He filled the sink
with suds, and started washing. Dishes flew
from tentacle to tentacle. No sooner had one
been picked up, than it was whisked across
the room for a scrub, then whirled onto the
top of a neat stack. Octopus had a gleaming
stack of twenty clean dishes before Angus

had finished one! It was like being inside a whirlwind, only with more soap and crockery. And a fishier smell.

Ten minutes later, the innkeeper came back and got the shock of his life. Every dish was sparkling!

"But how?" he gasped, handing over ten gold coins, as agreed.

"Don't forget about the hat," said Octopus, in Angus's voice.

"Oh yes, that's right." The innkeeper fetched a knife, a fork, a plate, and his flowery cap.

Angus went straight to the cobblers', and bought Octopus another pair of boots. "Why, thank you!" said the slimy creature.

The unlikely pair set off for the next town, in the hope of making more money. They hadn't been on the road long, when they saw the Princess' coach up ahead, being ambushed by armed robbers!

"We'd better hide!" said Angus.

"No way!" said Octopus, "They may be tough, but they're not as *well-armed* as me!"

The duo charged toward the robbers, and a second later, everything went dark.

Angus yelped, "I can't see!"

"I made an ink cloud," called Octopus, pulling a frying pan from Angus' satchel.

As the robbers blundered around, unable to see where they were going, Octopus bonked  them all on the head with the frying pan, then tied them up.

As the ink cloud cleared, the Princess stuck her head out of the coach window. "What a relief! Who should I thank for saving me?"

Octopus pointed four tentacles at Angus.

The Princess clasped her hands together and gazed into Angus' eyes. "My hero!"

"Oh, it was easy!" said Angus. Which, from his point of view, was absolutely true.

Meanwhile, news of Sir Loin's retirement had reached his old enemy, the ogre Gutrot. Gutrot was imprisoned in a cell, guarded by a knight called Sir Tenly Knot.

One morning, as Sir Tenly was tucking into a plate of dragon eggs, he heard a cry.

"Gosh!" bellowed Gutrot. "A treasure map! One that is most definitely real and not part of a trick!"

"Are you *sure* it's not a trick?" asked Sir Tenly, who wasn't the brightest gem in the treasure chest. "It's not like that time when you pretended to find a magic lamp, is it? Or the time when a beautiful princess came to visit, except that it turned out to be you in a cunning disguise?"

"No, it truly is a treasure map!"

"Wow!" said Sir Tenly. "May I see?"

Moments later, Gutrot was free, and Sir Tenly Knot was locked in the cell, wearing his dragon eggs on his head.

Gutrot made straight for the royal palace, kidnapped the King, and placed the crown on his own head.

"Bow to me, King Gutrot the Ghastly!"

The people of the kingdom quaked in fear at their new ruler, and begged for a hero to come over and vanquish him.

Edstrong decided he wanted to follow in Sir Loin's footsteps and defeat the ogre. He marched to the palace, brandishing his father's sword and shield. "Do your worst, ogre!" he yelled.

"Very well," grinned Gutrot, cracking his knuckles.

Moments later, Edstrong stumbled back out of the palace, with his sword wrapped around his neck, wondering how he got there.

When Anvil heard what had happened to Edstrong, she laughed. "My brother is a fool. There is only one woman for this job. "

When she arrived at the palace, she
yelled, "Do your worst, ogre!"

"I already did my worst," Gutrot pouted,
"when that other fellow came by earlier."

"Then do your *second* worst!" cried Anvil.

Gutrot laughed. "Alright then."

Anvil lowered her lance and charged into
the palace. Moments later, she charged right
back out again, with her lance tied in a knot.

When the news of his siblings' trials reached Angus, he couldn't help but feel a little bit smug. "It looks like Dad's gifts *really* helped them," he said, sarcastically.

"Why don't you have a go?" said Octopus.

Angus and Octopus walked to the palace. When they stopped outside, Octopus camouflaged himself against a hedge.

Gutrot peered over the battlements.

"Another one? And not even armed? What do *you* want?"

Angus whispered to Octopus, "I've changed my mind! I'll never beat him in a fight!"

"Don't worry," said Octopus, "Just challenge him anyway. I know one contest that he'll *never* win. Trust me on this one!"

Angus looked doubtful, but nonetheless he shouted, "I challenge you, O ogre!"

"To a talent contest!" Octopus yelled, mimicking Angus's voice. "And if I win, you must leave the throne and set the King free!"

"Deal!" Gutrot cried, eagerly.

"Really?" said Angus.

"Oh yes! I'm the undefeated champion of *The Big Spooky Forest Talent Show.*"

"Come back tomorrow, and we'll have our contest!" cried Gutrot. "In the meantime, I'll get everything set up."

"That didn't *quite* go to plan, did it?" said Angus, as he and Octopus trudged away.

When the pair returned to the castle the next day, they found its door wide open. A stage had been set up in the courtyard, and three strangely dressed wizards were sitting at a judges' table.

"You should be backstage, darling. Go and break a leg!" said one of them.

"I don't even *have* a leg," said Octopus, as he and Angus ducked around the curtain.

Spectators had begun to gather, and stallholders were selling them food. "Roll up, roll up! Get your rotten fruit and veggies!"

Angus gulped as he saw the crowd eagerly snapping up mushy old vegetables to throw.

"Don't give up now," said Octopus.

"But I don't even *have* a talent," said Angus.

"What, nothing?"

Angus shuffled his feet. "Well, I guess I can juggle."

Octopus grinned. "I can work with that."
As the curtains opened again, Octopus used
his camouflage abilities to blend into the
background. "Now—juggle for your life!"

Angus grabbed two handfuls of fruit
from a passing stallholder and began to
juggle. Octopus caught the fruit in his

tentacles, and tossed it
up again quickly. If
you didn't look
too closely, it
made it seem like
Angus was an
amazing juggler!
The crowd whooped
and cheered in
amazement.

At the end of the act, the judges held up
their scores. "Three golden cabbages," gasped
Angus. "They love me!"

Next, Gutrot strode in front of the crowd.

"Yes, juggling fruit is impressive," bellowed the ogre. "But wait until you get a load of my *extreme* juggling."

And with that, he started to juggle three horses. The crowd screamed with delight and the judges awarded Gutrot three golden cabbages, too!

"So ... what else have you got?" asked Gutrot, smiling a truly awful smile.

"What else *have* I got?" Angus yelped at Octopus backstage.

"There are some instruments back here," said the Octopus. "Can you play any?"

"I can play a few chords on the guitar," said Angus, "but it will take more than that to win a contest like this!"

Octopus thought for a moment. "I've got it!"

Moments later, Angus took to the stage, covered in instruments: a one-man band! He played a jolly tune and nobody in the crowd noticed the little tentacles snaking about to hit the drum or clash the cymbals.

The crowd loved it, and the judges awarded Angus three more golden cabbages.

Gutrot pushed past Angus onto the stage. "That was impressive—but wait until you hear this ballad, played upon my armpit."

By the time the ogre had finished making squelching noises, the whole audience was in floods of tears. "I have never heard anything so beautiful," sobbed one of the judges, as they again awarded Gutrot a top score.

The contest went on for the whole night. Gutrot matched Angus in opera singing, flower arranging, joke telling, and even baking!

"This is really heavy going," said Angus.

"Wait, that's it!" said Octopus. "Now I know what do to!" Moments later, Angus strode onto the stage, smiling broadly.

"Ladies and gentlemen, witches and wizards. My next talent will be a tap dance!"

He started to tap, faster and faster. It was a rhythm nobody in the kingdom had ever heard before! But what they didn't know was that Octopus was right next to the stage, tapping as fast as he could with his booted tentacles. At the end of the act, Angus strolled

off the stage to a standing ovation, and three
more golden cabbages.

Of course, Gutrot wasn't going to give up
easily. He leaped onto the stage and started
stamping about with his huge ogre feet.

STAMP, STAMP, STAMP, CRASH!

Gutrot had stamped a hole right through
the stage! The crowd howled with laughter.

The judges weren't impressed, and gave the ogre just one golden cabbage this time. The air filled with rotten vegetables as the crowd turned on him.

"I won!" Angus cried, turning to Gutrot. "Now you have to set the King free!"

Gutrot was furious, of course, but he kept his word. The King was set free, and his first order was to throw the ogre back in his deep, dark dungeon.

The Princess, who had been watching from the crowd, sidled up to Angus. "You saved me, and now you've saved the kingdom. Do you want to go on a date?

I know a lovely little seafood place." On hearing that, Octopus squeaked indignantly.

"That sounds great," said Angus, "but instead, how's about we drop by my local inn? They have *really* clean dishes!"

The King clapped Angus on the back. "I must give you a reward for saving me."

"Actually, Your Majesty," said Angus, "this octopus is the real hero."

"Is that so?" laughed the King. "Then what do you want, creature?"

Octopus smiled. "There is one thing. Well, eight actually … "

"You can have a hundred!"

And so, the King's cobbler was put to work, making a hundred shoes. Clogs! Platform boots! Winkle pickers! Snow shoes! Roller skates! And Octo-Puss in Boots became famous throughout the kingdom.